T0368457

The Oatmeal Club

Nasser Abuhamda

AuthorHouse™
1663 Liberty Drive
Bloomington, IN 47403
www.authorhouse.com

This book is printed on acid-free paper.

ISBN: 979-8-8230-3503-3 (sc)
ISBN: 979-8-8230-3504-0 (e)

Library of Congress Control Number: 2024920923

Print information available on the last page.

Published by AuthorHouse 10/09/2024

authorHOUSE®

A gang of kids with special disabilities, comes together with their leader Elon, who forms the oatmeal club, his purpose is to take control of the hospital by means of being scrupulous and devious at the same time. Using methods of blackmail, lies, and just plain random mischief. –

Elon then takes the gang to their competitors such as other children's hospitals, then expands out to other locations such as Sesame Street, schoolyards etc. the goal of Elon and his oatmeal club is to take advantage of their disabilities and show that nothing is too impossible or hold them down.

it is a beautiful day for the kids at a hospital for special disabilities, here they have enjoyed many years with the staff, but there is one kid that feels, he has much more potential, and sees himself with a greater role to play, he looks to himself as a leader for the kids, and tells them that they can overcome their disabilities by being active and showing their talents, however a very crafty character and very manipulative, he seeks power by deception, he looks for an opportunity to put his plan into action.

being very manipulative – he explains to them that they are being used by the hospital, and they have much more potential if they take control for themselves – and the only way is by following him.

sitting in the solarium he observes the kids, then makes his move – being very devious – he comes over to the kids and explains to them that, they might have disabilities but they can overcome this by being creative and to be independent – and the only way they can achieve this is to be active he then introduces himself.

Elon: – hello everyone, allow me to introduce myself – my name is Elon and I'm here to help you.

deceiving them, Elon then begins to ridicule the hospital as using them for commercials –

Elon: – listen up gang, I am Elon – and if you want to have your own money and more freedom, now is the time to start, and I can help you achieve that.

suddenly one kid tells the gang that – Elon is a liar, and what he really wants is power to take over the hospital by using the kids and their situation.

having one leg, the kid uses a crutch to help him stand, Elon then goes over to him.

Elon: – you seem to know me and my motive – either you are with us – or you are against us.

Elon – knowing that this kid will expose him to the doctors, goes over to confront the kid.

Elon: – hey kid – what's your name? – You sound like a smart kid, maybe you can join us.

suddenly, Elon pulls the crutch out from underneath him and the kid falls to the ground.

Elon: – that's for being the hospital's pet – ha ha ha

the kid, all surprised of what Elon had done, tells him that he will report Elon to the nurse.

Elon : – come on, I was just kidding, come on get up

Elon, knowing full well he can get into big trouble – approaches the kid and pretends to help him backup.

Elon: – oh come on – that was just a joke, let me help you up

suddenly Elon starts whacking the kid with his crutches

Elon: – this is what happens to snitches – and if you want to play hero, then there is plenty more for you – little hero.

After the beating – Elon tells the kid to kiss his hand – the kid all shaken up, does so out of fear

Elon: – let that be a lesson to you

making an example to other kids – Elon exalts himself and laughs sadistically.

Elon: – let that be a lesson – isn't that funny,,, a lesson – ha ha ha

he then organizes the kids, and creates his own little group

Elon: – hey listen kids, if you want to make money and go places – then follow me, from now on we meet in the solarium every Wednesday 9 AM, – I think we can call ourselves – the oatmeal club .

then one kid known as Lee asks Elon, how can we make money

Elon: – hey China – this is America, land of opportunity – just stick with me and we can all profit and enjoy the benefits.

the next day, as doctors are making their rounds – Elon pretends to be in pain

Elon: – the pain – the pain – Dr. I'm in pain, could I have something for the pain?

he then gets an idea, instead of taking it – he puts it into his drawer, where he will use them at a later time for a different purpose.

the next day, he tells the gang to do the same, and explains his idea.

Elon: – what I tell you, you must keep it a secret between us only, with the extra pain pills we can help other people – with pain problems – at the same time we can profit from our – humanitarian act.

suddenly, without warning – a nurse comes into the room and tells the kids to be ready for dinner. However, Elon is frozen in fear, thinking the nurse had overheard him.

Elon: – what – what was that? – – Yeah sure.

all shaken up, and sweating profusely, Elon rounds everyone up.

Elon: – now listen up – that was a close one, we have to organize ourselves, we must be a unit with lookouts and information teams.

okay Lisa, you will be my assistant in organizing matters, and Brian since you're good with computers we can use that to our benefit.

Elon: – Jeremy and Lee, you guys will be my backup, if we are going to be the oatmeal club, we must meet in the mornings and be organized.

later that day, Elon overhears two doctors discussing on having the kids making a play for the hospital. Elon noticing the opportunity, rushes back to the gang

being manipulative and fabricating lies, Elon tells the kids that the doctors don't really care about them, instead they use them. But Jeremy and Lee tells – Elon that they believe the doctors do care, and is doing the best for them – furious, Elon lashes out.

Elon: – care about us? – What are you smoking buddy, they never pay us for any shows we do.

However there is one doctor I must get out the way before he realizes my intentions.

Elon goes to his room, and grabs his cell phone, and a box of chocolate that his mother gave him, then wraps the chocolate with a letter stating – to my one and only, and perceives to the doctors office.

later at the nurses station, Elon goes into his act and pretends to not feeling well, then asks to see Dr. Whipple, The nurses very confused calls the doctor and starts checking on Elon.

not sure of what is wrong with Elon, the nurse takes his vital signs, then over to the doctors office.

as Dr. Whipple and the nurse goes through Elon's chart, Elon places the box of chocolate on to the doctors desk without him noticing.

suddenly – Elon trips the nurse over with his feet, having her fall right onto the doctor and knocking the chocolate down – Elon quickly snaps photos with his cell phone without any of them noticing.

as luck would have it, the nurse picks up the box and hands it over to the doctor – once again Elon snaps more photos.

knowing that he has the doctor and the nurse exactly how he planned it, Elon would now use it to his advantage at a later time.

later that evening, Elon goes over to the doctors office –

Elon: – hello Doc, would like to discuss some propositions if you don't mind. With all the plays that we do in this hospital, why aren't we being paid for it – I mean let's face it, making a play takes a lot of preparations and is very hard work.

the doctor very confused at Elon's question tells him that,

Dr.: – the hospital is very grateful for any plays that the kids do, and we try our best with all the kids needs, but we really don't pay anyone, any donations to the hospital goes directly in helping the kids with their needs.

Elon: – look doc, we can do much better if we go and perform somewhere else, such as Broadway where we can have a much larger crowd, not to mention more money.

Elon: – actually, we can do much better on our own, and get paid a lot more than what the hospital can give out.

surprised at Elon's discussion – the doctor questions Elon's motive

Dr.: – look Elon, you are getting out of line, and only the hospital can approve of any performances. By the way what is the purpose of all this, and where do you get this idea of – making money from? – This is a hospital where we do our best in taking care of patients like yourself.

Elon then pressures the doctor

Elon: – look doc – you asked me, what is my purpose and my answer is – free enterprise – Unless of course you're a communist.

Dr.: – that's enough – it is Dr. Whipple – not Doc, and no I'm not a communist –, so I suggest you stop this nonsense and get back to your room.

Elon: – whatever you say Dr. – and yes, I do feel a little tired – I think I'll head back to bed, it's been a long day, however I do believe will meet again concerning this matter.

the next day, Elon is in the lobby when suddenly, he overhears the conversation with a kid and his parents complaining to the nursing staff, about the pain medication that is not working too well – Elon takes the opportunity and approaches them.

Elon: – hey daddyo – couldn't help overhearing, but I hear you have a problem, and I think I can help you with that.

the father all confused asks Elon

father: – who are you? – are you pushing drugs?

Elon: – what me – a drug pusher – no way – I'm a patient here, just like your son – but I think I can help with your problem.

Elon: – Here, have Junior try some and let me know how they work.

Elon then goes over to the gang with an idea.

Elon – hey gang listen up, each of us gets pain pills, now we don't need most of them, so I suggest we sell the extras, and help people with pain problems.

then one of the kids confronts Elon about the pills.

kid: – but Elon, isn't that illegal?

Elon: – what? – Me – What do you mean?

all nervous and sweating – Elon convinces the gang that, the kid is only jealous and trying to steal his idea – the gang then yells out to the kid, and tells him – he is just jealous of Elon, and that he just wants to help everyone. kids : – Elon is right, he's only trying to help – why are you bothering him – leave Elon alone.

Elon – knowing that he has the gang on his side, starts laughing sadistically

Elon: – ha ha ha – I have them in my control.

days later – Elon is at the lobby once again – but then he notices the custodian holding his back in pain. He then goes over to him.

Elon: – here grandpa, I notice you're in pain, maybe I can help – take some of these, and you will feel much better – however there is a price

Elon: – if you need more – or maybe your friends, you can always find me in the solarium, I'll be there every Friday at 3 PM – let's just say it'll be our little secret.

as the days go by, many of the custodians come over to Elon for their problems –

making money – and loving every minute of it – Elon gets an idea.

he then goes over to the gang and explains his idea of how they can make money, but also how he can expand his operation.

Elon: – that's right – we can make money and help people at the same time – of course I will have to get a percentage of what we make, since it's my idea.

Jeremy all concerned about the actions, confronts Elon

Jeremy: – but isn't this illegal, and what good is it making money, when were still in the hospital

Elon: – what – are you a communist ? – look buckwheat – you don't know what you're talking about, we have a gold mine here and if we play it right, we can make really big bucks.

Elon: – and what do you mean illegal – doctors push this stuff every day – and about the hospital we can buy our own homes – for our families, cars to travel – and finally get out of this dump.

as the days go by – Elon expands his operation, this time using the gang, janitors come over to him on a weekly basis, loving every minute of it – Elon sits and collects – making him a very wealthy kid.

then one day, Elon notices that his commission is getting a little light. Frustrated he calls the gang for a meeting and tells them to meet him in the solarium and to sit in a circle.

later that day, the gang gathers in the solarium – then Elon comes in with two chobby kids as his personal bodyguards – Elon discusses, teamwork, unity and loyalty, he then carries a wiffleball bat and starts going around the gang yelling – teamwork – teamwork

Elon: – when I started this operation, I thought we had an agreement to work together as a team – and a team plays together – as a team.

Elon: – but as I count my bag, I find it a little light and that means someone isn't playing a fair game.

Elon: – the only way we can have teamwork, is if everyone is on the same team

suddenly, he starts whacking lee

Elon: – this is for being greedy – Mr. Lee – just because you lost the war, doesn't mean you can take my money.

Elon: – this is my operation, if we are a team we must act like one.

Elon: – it's time we expand and make our own Mark – and we can use some of the custodians for distribution to other hospitals where they can pass it on to other custodians, this way we can relieve their pain with our products.

as Elon is talking to the gang – a commercial comes on promoting another hospital for children

Elon: – look you see – other hospitals are making commercials, and what do they do to us – they make us put on a play in front of our own hospital staff – what kind of treatment is that?

Elon then plays a scare tactic on the gang – to encourage them that they must take action.

Elon: – look gang, if we don't get our act together, we will be on welfare – and you know what that means – – – leftovers for dinner – dirty sheets – and no PlayStation.

Elon: – we have to come up with a plan to make the other hospital look bad – such as kids falling off beds – patience not being attended to – and tasteless food – – which wouldn't be hard to do.

Elon: – the media would be a great start to getting our attention – and you know how – the media loves bad news – also, social media – Facebook – twitter – Insta Graham – this will be a great opportunity for us to promote our hospital as being a better choice, not to mention more donations.

as Elon starts putting his plan together, Brian and Lisa comes over

Brian: – Elon, I've gotten through to the patient portal from the other hospital, we can now make comments as how bad the hospital is, and make comments of the treatments on their page.

Lisa: – we can tell stories of patients being abandoned.

as Elon's plans comes together, he is very excited to have come this far
Elon: – excellent – everything is coming to plan, ha ha ha

Elon then prepares the gang to make their final preparations to expose the other hospital – but also to promote his.

Elon: – okay gang listen up, Mike and Lee your role is to cause distraction– everyone else knows there roll.

Jeremy: – but Elon, how can we get pass the staff at the door?

Elon: – I will take care of that – meet me downstairs at 6 o'clock, that's around dinnertime, and the staff will have their hands full. Brian will call an uber that is wheelchair accessible – once the cab is here – we all leave together.

as Elon gets ready, he starts painting himself with black paint as a commando going on a raid

Jeremy: – what's that for

Elon: – don't you know anything – it's like an Army Ranger going behind enemy lines

Elon: – I don't think you will need any – right?

at 6 o'clock sharp – Elon goes over to a fire alarm box – then pulls the handle.

With the alarm ringing, he rushes to the door and out to where the uber van is waiting along with the gang.

as Elon jumps inside – he tells the gang

Elon: – okay everyone, you know what to do when we get there – don't mess up

Elon: – okay Gandhi – what are you waiting for – let's go.

later as they arrive at the hospital – Elon tells them to get into position before the news crew arrives.

Elon: – Lee, take the glasses and pretend you're blind, let's make this look good

as the news crew arrives, they are stunned to see the gang all over the place

With Elon lying flat on the ground – gargling.

Elon: – help – I've fallen and can't get up

with all the distraction going on, Lisa with Jeremy and Brian runs into the hospital unnoticed

as the news crew approaches Elon, he goes straight into his act.

Elon: – water - water – can anyone give me water –AAHH.

reporter: – what's your name kid, and what happened here?

Elon: – is the camera on – good – let's keep it at profile okay.

reporter: – we've got a call that, some kids were being unattended to – and abandoned –

is this true and are you one of them?

Elon: – of course I am – what do you think I'm doing here.

reporter: – why would they do this?

Elon: – RACISM

reporter: – racism? – But there are multicultural groups of kids in this hospital

Elon: – and you believe them?

reporter: – how long has this been going on?

Elon: – oh – it's been so long – I can't remember, the horror that goes on behind those walls, is unimaginable

Elon: – look, they even abandoned the blind

reporter: – oh my God, what happened to you, are you all right?

Lee: – he
lp – I can't see, – food – do you have any chocolate on you?

Elon angry with Lee's – chocolate remarks – takes the stick and starts whacking Lee.
Elon: – tell them – water dummy.

the news crew then starts the interview – and Elon steps right in.

Elon: – it's madness I tell you – dirty sheets – dirty underwear's – and would you believe it –no Netflix !

Elon: – come, follow me and I'll show you

Elon leads the news crew into the hospital – Lisa with Jeremy and Brian spills soup all over each other – and lays on the floor as if they are homeless

reporters: – oh my God – look at them, they all look homeless and neglected

as they enter the hospital – the staff is very surprised and shocked to see all of the cameras and the news crew coming in.

Elon: – as you can see, the staff are hiding in shame

suddenly the hospitals supervisor confronts the news crew

supervisor: – what is the meaning of this, what are the cameras for? – And who are these kids?

Elon then goes into his act as if he is frightened

Elon: – there he is – it's him – it's the master – please don't let him hurt me

all confused of Elon's screams – the doctors along with the news crew, looks on in confusion.

Elon: – the horror – the horror –ahhhh

the reporter – thinking Elon is traumatized, pulls him away from the supervisor – leaving the supervisor all confused.

reporter: – Elon, can you tell us what goes on in the hospital.

Elon: – can't you see the kids laying on the floor – can you imagine, no McDonald's, no Burger King for our meals – Not even Wendy's.

the reporter then tells Elon to make some comments about the hospital – on camera Elon taking the opportunity, and starts promoting his hospital as a better choice.

Elon: – hey kids – if you're like me, and want better treatmet – call – Joseph's Hospital for kids – they take care of you much better just call – 800 – 555 – kids – – and don't forget about the donations.

later at Joseph's hospital – everyone is watching

kids: – hey look Elon is on TV

later that evening as Elon and the gang gets back to their hospital, the doctors discusses the situation with Elon in his office.

Dr.: – what was this whole thing about – and what did you mean by – the hospital holding you hostage? – You're not even a patient there Do you know we can be in big trouble for this?

Elon: – relax – relax – look at it this way Doc – we eliminated our competition, and now we are number one – in Children's hospitals choice !

Dr. Whipple: – first of all it's Dr. Whipple – not Doc second – you had no right to do what you did – also there has been rumors going around about painkillers being sold,, we believe that it might be one of the custodians doing this – and since you and the oatmeal club pretty much run things here, would you have any idea as to who it might be?

Elon starts shaking very nervously

Elon: – what painkillers? – Who what me? – I mean – what happened? – Who did what? –

all sweaty and nervous – the doctor tries to calm Elon down

Dr.: – relax Elon, relax – what's wrong with you?

Elon – very relieved that they did not suspect him for selling the painkillers – then gets into his act

Elon: – I think I had a long day Dr. – I need some rest.

as the next day comes around, Elon is in bed with breakfast, suddenly a nurse rushes in and states to Elon
nurse: – Elon, there are some reporters here to see you – also doctors and hospital officials – looks like you're very popular now.

Elon: – what do you mean?

nurse: – the media loved how you promoted our hospital – they're asking you to do some commercials – with you as the leading spokesperson for the hospital, the doctors are in a conference now, but will meet you in the lobby with the media.

Elon: – well, is that so – give me five minutes

meanwhile, before making an interview with the media, the doctors are discussing the situation about Elon and the other hospital.

Dr. Whipple: – this Elon is a very inquisitive kid, he seems to get his nose into everything – I believe he's also the leader to a group they call – the oatmeal club, they're a very troublesome bunch.

administrator: – what do you mean by that – he's done us a big favor and managed to get the attention of the medical institutions to promote our hospital – without him we would still be in the red.

Dr. Whipple: –: but you don't know him, he can be very unpredictable and very manipulative.

as the doctors continue the discussion – Elon just so happens to be strolling along and overhears the conversation.

Elon: – huh, what's this?

Dr. Whipple: – don't underestimate Elon, he always has something up his sleeve – I don't trust him, maybe we should use another kid for the commercial.

Administrator: – nonsense – the media loves him and we need him for the commercial, he'll be a great asset for the hospital.

later, as Elon arrives at the lobby – he is met buy the media with cameras, flashing lights, and reporters, along with the kids from the hospital yelling – Elon, Elon, Elon!

the institution for Children's Hospital and the media, all gather around Elon to make some statements.

Administrator: – today is a proud moment for us, to have our hospital to be picked out as one of the best hospitals for children, and today we proudly announce that we will have a special child who will become our ambassador, to represent the hospital – and that is – Elon Strauss

Elon: – thank you my public, and today I accept your nomination for me being your – ambassador – and I will assure you, we will be the number one Children's Hospital.

with the kids applauding – Jeremy tries to get into the picture– Elon then trips him, with Jeremy falling to the ground.

one reporter asks Elon, what would he propose for his hospital as an ambassador –

Elon: – as ambassador – I will make my hospital – – great again! Ha ha ha ha

after the ceremony, the doctors meet with Elon in the conference room to discuss his role as the ambassador, Elon then grabs a cigar – and states

Elon: – hello gentlemen – we have lots to discuss!

Dr. Knoll: – what's the cigar for – you know you cant do that –

Elon: – well, the way I see it – I am the ambassador now, and I think we should consider my position – also we must discuss about having my own office.

Dr. Whipple: – I don't think that will be necessary, I think we should reconsider this whole thing.

Elon: – You see Dr. Knoll – – Dr. pimple has been harassing me for a long time, and now that I was appointed ambassador – he's jealous.

Dr. Knoll – first of all he's Dr. Whipple, not pimple – second what's this jealousy and harassment – is this true Dr. Whipple?

Dr. Whipple: – of course not, I told you he is trouble, and if we keep him as ambassador – he will hijack the hospital.

Elon then goes into his act – starts shaking like he's having a convulsion

Elon: – what? – did you hear that – now he's threatening me. – I must have protection.

Dr. Knoll: – now that's enough – from the both of you, I want everyone in full compliance and working together – our hospital is now going to be everywhere with commercials, and parents calling in.

We must be ready for that, and expanding the hospitals potential.

Elon then makes a statement that will shift the balance of power

Elon: – I think – Dr. pimple will always resent me – and for that matter – he might hurt me

Dr. Whipple: – no – you see – this is what I mean – he is an instigator and a trouble maker, Elon must not be put on as ambassador to this hospital.

after the conference Dr. Knoll warns Dr. Whipple about his anger towards Elon

Dr. Knoll: – I had enough of your anger – you are not to present yourself in an unprofessional manner leave Elon alone – and that's an order.

Dr. Whipple: – but I did not do anything – he's manipulating you.

Elon then pretends he is being attacked, then gets Dr. Knoll on his side

Dr. Whipple: – I am a doctor in this hospital, and I will not allow him as ambassador.

Elon: – help – help me – he's coming after me

Dr. Knoll: – Dr. Whipple that's enough – stop attacking him – or I'll call the security

After the conference – Elon is met by a cheering crowd

Elon: – thank you – thank you my fellow Americans – as I stated – we have just begun, and we will prevail against any unconstitutional acts against us.

Crowd: – yay – Elon – Elon – Elon – yay – yay – yay

Elon: – we now have – better food, – better service –, and yes – – pizza and Netflix !

Crowd – Elon – Elon – Elon!!!

Lisa: – Elon you did it – we now have everything we need!

Elon: – no – not everything – not yet

Lisa: – what do you mean – thanks to you, we now have less restrictions and more freedoms!

Elon: – yes, we have many things now – but now we must expand – expand our brand

and that means – commercials – holiday specials – and our bank accounts!

Elon: – if we don't be careful, another hospital will try and steal our position – and I'm not going to let that happen.

A couple of days later, the kids notice that they are not allowed to go out, pizza orders has been stopped – the kids then turn to Elon for help.

Kids: – Elon, they stopped us from going out – and they cut off our pizza

Elon: – what – no pizza!

Elon then takes advantage of the situation and rallies the kids behind him – with a fiery speech

Elon: – Dr. Whipple did this– This is our hospital – our parents paid taxes – we have our patients rights – we have the Bill of Rights – we have the Constitution!

we are Americans – and we are free – free – I told you before Dr. Whipple is a closet communist, and you know how they work.

kids: – yay – yay – yay – USA – USA – USA

Elon: – I will confront this Dr. Whipple – I believe he is jealous of us, and do you know why? – Because we are now in the limelight of this hospital – and more popular than he is – but I also believe he has bad intentions – it is always those who have the power – love to oppress others.

Elon: – do you want to live in the darkness of slavery – with no rights in a locked down society – told what to do –

Elon: – or – do you want to live free – and bask in the sunshine of freedom? – – I say advance – into the sunshine of freedom!

kids: – freedom – freedom !!! –

Elon: – I say advance – advance in the sunshine of freedom

kids: – freedom – freedom – USA – USA – USA

Elon: – I don't know about you, but I'm an American – I have my rights – and I will confront Dr. Whipple – and let our voices be heard!

Kids: – Elon – Elon – Elon !!!

later, Elon is in Dr. Whipple's office along with Lisa and lee, and tells them to video the conference.

Elon: – Dr. Whipple, may we have a word with you?

Elon: – why have we been deprived of our rights – and why has our pizza orders been stopped?

Dr. Whipple: – you have not been deprived of your rights Elon, it's too cold outside, second – you can't have pizza every day – that's not healthy

Elon: – oh look, now he's working for the UN – why not just put a huge electric fence around our hospital – comrade!

Dr. Whipple: – what are you insinuating Elon? – These are the rules, and we have responsibility for taking care of everyone in the hospital

Dr. Whipple: – I don't know what you are trying to do – but this has to stop, you are meddling into hospitals affairs – and that is where I come in.

Elon: – need I remind you that, I am the ambassador – and I must have say into this.

Dr. Whipple: – now that's enough – you are way out of line, – if you keep this up, you'll be notified to the administration office.

Elon: – whatever you say comrade.

Dr. Whipple: – what?

Dr. Whipple, now very angry, calls the nurse and security to take him back to his room

Dr. Whipple: – that's it – I am calling the security to escort you back to your room

Just before the security arrives – Elon takes out his cell phone, and sends the photos showing where the nurse had accidentally fallen onto Dr. Whipple with the chocolates.

Dr. Whipple: – what is this –?

Elon: – let's just say – Mrs. Whipple wouldn't like to see you giving a pretty nurse – some lovely chocolates for Valentines.

Dr. Whipple: – this is black male – you little degenerate!

suddenly as Dr. Knoll arrives with the nurses and security – Elon throws himself on the floor

Elon: – oh my arm – my legs – help, help – I'm being attacked!

Dr. Knoll: – what is the meaning of this – what are you doing to him

Dr. Whipple – all nervous, starts shaking and sweating – confronts Dr. Knoll

Dr. Whipple: – he's a liar – this guy is a psychopath – he's mentally disturbed

Elon: – gargling on the floor

the security guard picks up Elon from the floor, believing he was thrown down

Elon – the horror,,, oh the horror

Dr. Whipple: – I didn't touch him, he threw himself down on his own – he's a psychopath

As Dr. Whipple is escorted away – yelling and screaming, Elon discusses matters with Dr. knoll

Elon: – I think Dr. Whipple has been working too hard, maybe he should take a vacation.

Dr. knoll: – yes, I believe you're right, we will see what we can do about that.

Dr. Whipple: – the kid is insane, don't trust him – he's nothing but trouble and a liar

Dr. Knoll: – don't worry Elon, I will take care of this, I will have an investigation on Dr. Whipple

Elon: – thank you Dr. Knoll – you're a true American!

Dr. Knoll: – I know this has been hard on you Elon, can we get you anything

Elon: – well actually yes,,, if it's not a problem, can I have some pizza ?

Ha ha ha – ha ha ha

The end

Printed in the United States
by Baker & Taylor Publisher Services